Labracadabra

by Jessie Nelson
& Karen Leigh Hopkins

illustrated by Deborah Melmon

Viking

An Imprint of Penguin Group (USA) Inc.

Viking

Published by Penguin Group

Penguin Young Readers Group, 345 Hudson Street, New York, New York 10014, U.S.A.

Penguin Group (Canada), 90 Eglinton Avenue East, Suite 700, Toronto, Ontario,
Canada M4P 2Y3 (a division of Pearson Penguin Canada Inc.)

Penguin Books Ltd, 80 Strand, London WC2R 0RL, England

Penguin Ireland, 25 St Stephen's Green, Dublin 2, Ireland
(a division of Penguin Books Ltd)

Penguin Group (Australia), 250 Camberwell Road, Camberwell, Victoria 3124,
Australia (a division of Pearson Australia Group Pty Ltd)

Penguin Books India Pvt Ltd, 11 Community Centre, Panchsheel Park,
New Delhi – 110 017, India

Penguin Group (NZ), 67 Apollo Drive, Rosedale, North Shore 0632, New Zealand
(a division of Pearson New Zealand Ltd.)

Penguin Books (South Africa) (Pty) Ltd, 24 Sturdee Avenue, Rosebank,
Johannesburg 2196, South Africa

Penguin Books Ltd, Registered Offices: 80 Strand, London WC2R 0RL, England

First published in 2011 by Viking, a division of Penguin Young Readers Group

1   3   5   7   9   10   8   6   4   2

Text copyright © Jessie Nelson and Karen Leigh Hopkins, 2011
Illustrations copyright © Deborah Melmon, 2011
All rights reserved

LIBRARY OF CONGRESS CATALOGING-IN-PUBLICATION DATA
Nelson, Jessie.
Labracadabra / by Jessie Nelson & Karen Leigh Hopkins ; illustrated by
Deborah Melmon.
p. cm.
Summary: Zach always wanted a dog but Larry, the full-grown mongrel
his parents choose, is not it, however, he soon discovers that there is
something very special—even magical—about Larry's tail.
ISBN 978-0-670-01251-0 (hardcover)
[1. Dogs—Fiction. 2. Human-animal relationships—Fiction. 3. Magic—Fiction.] I.
Hopkins, Karen Leigh. II. Melmon, Deborah, ill.
III. Title.

PZ7.N4339Lab 2011   [E]—dc22   2010025109

Manufactured in China   Set in Egyptienne   Book design by Nancy Brennan

This book is dedicated to our firstborn pups,

the beautiful Molly June and Milly Rose

—J.N. & K.L.H.

For my sweet angel, Gracie—D.M.

I KNOW IT SOUNDS crazy. But really, it happened.

It all began around 11:32 last Tuesday.

My parents told me they had a surprise for me. They said it was something I had wanted for a long time. It wasn't my birthday or anything. And I didn't remember that I'd done anything special to have earned a surprise. Though sometimes my mom says I don't have to do anything special, I just am special. But then when she gets mad at me she'll say, "You may be special, but don't forget everyone is special," so go figure.

Back to the day.

My neighbor Molly Rose was babysitting. We used to be good friends and hang out in my tree house and play restaurant, but now she's a teenager. All she does is talk on the phone with her boyfriend. Mom says it's just a phase and that she really likes me, but I'm not sure.

My mom said, "Molly can help you clean up your room while we're gone." It seemed kind of unfair having to clean up while I waited for a surprise, but I didn't want to push it, because that's when my mom's left eyebrow goes up and you know you've gone too far.

The last time my parents said they had a surprise for me, they brought home a canoe and we took my cousin Seymour out on the lake. He threw up. Not to be mean, but I was hoping this new surprise didn't include him.

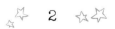

I searched the house for clues. None. Zip.

I was in the middle of my third peanut butter sandwich when my parents' car pulled up. I looked out the window and saw my mom sitting in the backseat. That was odd.

Then my dad yelled out, "Close your eyes." Just as I started to close my right eye, I nearly got trampled by something.

A DOG?! I'D ALWAYS WANTED A DOG! For like my entire life! I looked down at the dog, my new best friend. 'Cause that's what they say: "A dog is a man's best friend." And I didn't have a best friend.

But this dog was kind of big for a small dog and kind of small if you like big dogs, with a very large nose for a dog, and nostrils that were, like, huge. And his tail! His tail was really long and wagged in this really, really annoying way.

"What kind of dog is it?" I asked, trying to hide my disappointment.

"It's a little bit of everything. Part Labrador, part Brittany spaniel, part cadoodle, part dachshund, and maybe a little bit terrier," my dad said.

Dachshund? Cadoodle? Oh, brother. I had wanted a German shepherd or a golden retriever or a chocolate Lab. Not "a little bit of everything" with big nostrils and a weird tail. Well, maybe he'll grow into those.

"He's full grown, Zach," my mom said. "He's had a very hard life, so be really nice and welcome him into our home."

Hard life? I didn't want to feel sorry for my dog. I wanted a dog I could be proud of. A big dog. A tough dog. A smart dog. Not a used dog.

The dog looked up at me, wagging that tail.

I tried to cheer myself up. Maybe it would be a little fun to name it.

"He already has a name," my mom said. "And I think we should keep that name so he doesn't get confused."

Okay, what's the point of having a dog if you don't even get a chance to name it?

"What's his name?" I said, preparing myself for the worst.

"Larry."

"LARRY?!!!!" Larry was the kid who sat behind me in science and built an underwater volcano that exploded all over my desk. "Larry" was not a dog's name. A dog's name was supposed to be "Max" or "Mac" or "Rex." I would have even taken "Buddy." But Larry?? I vowed I'd never say it out loud.

I could hear Molly trying not to laugh.

Thanks, Mom. Thanks, Dad. Thanks, Larry. I started to walk away, but the dog—you notice I'm not saying "Larry"—stopped me with his tail.

"Ooh . . . He wants you to take him for a walk!" Mom said.

"Maybe later," I said. "I have to go clean my room first."

I KNOW IT SOUNDS crazy, but it happened around 10:15 last Thursday.

My dog and I were taking a walk, just down the block, not so far that I couldn't see my house. My mother was on the porch. I could tell from her left eyebrow that she was still mad at me from her having told me to clean my room and me pushing everything under my bed, including the chocolate pudding from when my cousin Seymour was over. It didn't help that my underwear happened to fall in my goldfish bowl. The goldfish lived, which proves that underwear doesn't kill goldfish, but that's another story.

We started walking. My dog's weirdo tail was wagging so much, so fast, that Mom couldn't help laughing. My dog shot me a look. I could tell he was as relieved as I was that my mom's left eyebrow had gone back where it belonged.

Just as I was beginning to feel my own tail wag, there he was.

That kid—the tall one, like taller than all of us, like tree tall—who moved into the neighborhood from Arizona. He had no friends, and Mom said that's why he was so mean and we had to forgive him.

He reached for my dog's tail—it felt like he was going to pull it off and hit me with it. But before I could grab his hand, my dog started moving his tail in these wild figure

eights. I'm not kidding, almost like karate moves, like kung fu but cooler—like dog fu.

The kid didn't have a chance. Me, I just kept on walking, and when I turned around that tree-tall kid had shrunk as small as a potted plant.

I looked down at my dog. For the first time,

I started to think that my dog's tail might not be just a regular tail. It might be something more.

That night my dog went to sleep in the den on the new dog bed my mom had bought on sale at Dogs "R" Us. It was purple plaid, which I thought might make it hard for him to fall asleep. I turned off the light—he kind of looked at me like, "So this is how it works? You go upstairs and I stay down here alone on this big plaid purple pillow, with the sound of the ice maker going on and off all night?" But I just went upstairs and got into bed.

I had sheets with clouds on them, and I kept thinking of my dog trying to sleep sur-rounded by all that purple plaid. Just as I was closing my eyes, I heard a thump in the hallway. Like someone was knocking on my door, except that it wasn't closed.

It was my dog's tail thumping on the floor.

He was standing in the doorway staring at me. I knew that look. It was like the one my cousin Seymour gave me when he wanted me to invite him to sleep over.

But at that moment my mom called from her bedroom, "Larry! Downstairs—back to your own bed!" She is nutty on the subject of a good night's sleep. She says it totally makes or breaks your next day.

My dog's tail went droopy. He obediently turned around and headed downstairs. I heard his paws on the stairway till he settled on his bed with a thump of his tail.

I drifted off to sleep thinking about that tail. . . .

There was something about that tail. . . .

3

IT HAPPENED AT 11:22 two days later.

I was waiting for my cousin Seymour to come over so we could go to the beach. Cousin Seymour was nineteen minutes late, probably because he was overstuffing his backpack as usual. He was always bringing stuff over "in case." Like in case he got hungry for nuts, which he was allergic to, he would bring rice cakes, which had a flavor like kettle corn.

Cousin Seymour was allergic to every-thing, and sometimes I thought I was allergic to Cousin Seymour. He had all forty-four presidents' birthdays memorized, and I know it shouldn't but that got on my nerves. My mom said he was just "sensitive" and that children like Cousin Seymour often grew up to be fascinating adults.

But for now, all I could think about was the time he was eating soy cottage cheese because he was allergic to ice cream, and a big curd attached itself to his upper lip, and I had to stare at that curd the whole time, because we were in the back of the car together and I didn't want to say anything because I was afraid it would hurt his feelings because he was so sensitive.

That morning I'd just wanted to sit on the couch and watch TV with my dog. But his tail had been wagging like crazy, knocking over everything. First it was my box of Lucky

Charms, then it was my bowl, and it was the last of the Lucky Charms, and Mom said no she would not get me another box.

My dog started barking. He thought he had seen a ghost, but it was just Cousin Seymour getting out of the car, ghost white from the gobs of sunblock his mom made him wear. I wondered why he had put the sunblock on now, but Cousin Seymour said, "You're supposed to. You can read the directions."

Cousin Seymour played everything by the book. He always read all the directions, and

they did say to put it on at least fifteen minutes prior to being in the sun. So technically he was right. But I didn't like the way he always said, "You're supposed to," about everything.

Cousin Seymour looked at my dog. He didn't say, "What a great dog," or, "He looks so smart," or even, "What tricks does he do?" He just looked at him. That made me want to throw something at him. But I didn't. My mom said, "Before anything else happens, let's just get in the car."

I was glad my dog sat between me and Cousin Seymour, so that none of his sunblock would rub off on my leg. Miraculously, Cousin Seymour wasn't allergic to dogs.

I wished I'd been able to bring someone else, like my friend Brandon, especially when Cousin Seymour started listing all the different dog breeds my dog might be a mix of. About the time he named the 111th breed, including the Chinese crested and the Norwegian lundehund, Mom called out from the front seat, "See, didn't I tell you? Isn't he fascinating?"

Not to me.

Cousin Seymour began to eat his rice cakes that tasted like kettle corn. The car went around a really windy bend, and with no warning he threw up his rice cake.

I rolled down the window to get some air, because the smell of the sunblock and the throw up was getting too much for me.

Suddenly a bee flew in my window and went for Cousin Seymour. Cousin Seymour began to scream, "Oh no! I'm allergic to bees! I'm allergic to bees!" He looked really scared. I tried to swat the bee off him, but I was a little scared too. It kept flying near his nose, maybe because that was where a lot of the sunblock was. But now Cousin Seymour wasn't white anymore, he was red as a tomato and shaking like a bobble-head doll.

My mom was waving a rolled-up news-

paper behind her head, but it kept hitting Cousin Seymour in the face and missing the bee, who seemed to be getting madder and madder—buzzing really loud and flying in crazy circles around Cousin Seymour's head.

And that's when it happened. 12:09.

My dog wound up his tail like that great pitcher on the Yankees, and with one gigantic swoosh knocked the bee off Cousin Seymour's nose, past me, and right out the window.

Cousin Seymour hugged my dog. "This is the greatest dog in the world!" he said. That made me feel pretty good. If someone as smart and fascinating as Cousin Seymour said that, it must be true.

That's when I began to think my dog's tail wasn't a tail at all.

Maybe it was a magic wand.

IT HAPPENED AGAIN. AT 1:29 on Wednesday.

I had been invited to my new friend Brandon's birthday party. I'd always wanted a best friend, and Brandon had real best-friend potential. First, he had no allergies. Next, he was a great baseball player. Plus he wasn't afraid of the dark. Not to mention he had a giant trampoline in his backyard.

The birthday party was at 1:30. My mom had said I looked tired, plus I had a bad sunburn from my day at the beach with Cousin

Seymour, which had turned out to be really fun because we kept throwing a stick in the water and my dog would fetch it and bring it back by bodysurfing the wave no matter how far out we threw it.

Mom told me to rest before the party, so I climbed up to my tree house and lay down on the old air mattress with no air in it. There was a cool breeze and a weird tinkling from the wind chimes, and I fell asleep.

My mom thought I had gone to my room, so when it came time to wake me up for the party she went in there. She thought I was that big lump on the bed, but when she shook it she realized that it was just my covers all bunched up from where I had forgotten to make it that morning. I'm glad I wasn't there, because I'm sure her left eyebrow went up.

She said she called my name really loud.

But it must not have been that loud, 'cause I didn't hear it. She said she looked everywhere. Her room. The den. As if I would have slept on that purple plaid dog bed.

My dog watched her. She knew how important this birthday party was for me, for my future in the neighborhood. And somehow my dog did, too.

1:28.

Just as my mom was getting really worried, he ran out to the backyard. Took one sniff and hatched a plan. I know if he could have, he would have climbed up the tree and licked my face, or told my mom I was up there, but he couldn't speak English.

So there I am, fast asleep in this dream of jumping up into the clouds on Brandon's trampoline, when suddenly I hear what sounds like a drum solo. I mean it was wild—better

than any rock concert. Not that I've been to one, but I could tell that it was better. It woke me right up.

And when I looked down from the tree house to see who was playing, there was my dog banging his tail on the trash cans like they were bongos. What a tail! That tail really rocked.

With one minute to go, I jumped down from the tree. My mom was so happy to see me, she started crying. Moms do funny things like that sometimes.

My dog's tail pushed me out the front door and down the block just as Brandon's mom was hanging the balloons on the mailbox. I was the first to get there. I could tell Brandon was relieved 'cause you always get afraid no one will show up at your birthday party. Even Brandon.

Brandon and I ran to his trampoline. Just the two of us on it before the rest of the crowd got there. I was jumping to touch the clouds when I saw my dog's tail as it left Brandon's yard and headed toward my house. It was wagging. He had gotten me there right on time.

That's when I knew.

If this was a multiple choice test and I could check

MAYBE MY DOG'S TAIL IS A MAGIC WAND,

or

FOR SURE MY DOG'S TAIL IS A MAGIC WAND,

I would check FOR SURE.

That night in bed I was thinking about my dog in his purple plaid bed in the den below me.

Suddenly I heard a *clunk* on the stairs. I looked out my door, and I saw my dog dragging his purple plaid bed up the stairs. He finally got it up after like an hour and put it at the top of the stairs where he could see me. He was smart. I knew it would be easier to sleep when I could see him, too.

Thump. His tail on the hardwood floor. Good night to you, too, Larry.

That's when it hit me. Maybe it was all those breeds that Larry was made up of that made him so special. Larry was no ordinary mutt. Larry was a Labracadabra!

I T HAPPENED AGAIN THE next Sunday at 3:40 when I was swimming.

You remember Brandon, the kid with the most potential to be my best friend? We had really hung out at his birthday party, but then his older cousins came and did double back flips on the trampoline and he forgot about me.

He was at my house, and I could tell he was getting a little bored. We were having a hard time figuring out what to do next, but I didn't want him to go

home. We'd even had a double chocolate ice cream cone, but it hadn't done any good.

Just then my dog jumped into the pool. He started swimming so fast—like a motorboat—that you couldn't even see him. He was all tail. Brandon started laughing. Then my dog's tail started wagging in circles like the wheel of my bike when I'm going a hundred

miles an hour. And suddenly Brandon shouted, "Look! A rainbow!" And sure enough the spray from his tail was making a rainbow the whole length of the pool—and it's a big pool. Brandon said, "Your dog is so cool. Do you mind if I tell my mother I'll be home later?" My dog looked at me. He held his tail up, like thumbs up, and we both knew Brandon was a lock for best friend.

That night after Brandon left—yeah, he even stayed for dinner—my dog was exhausted. My mother said I should get ready for bed. I wasn't even tired, but I lay down on my bed. My dog came right in without even stopping in the doorway and lay down on the floor next to me.

It was hard for me to lie still. I wanted to see what other kind of magic his tail could do. But I knew I didn't have a lot of wiggle

room with Mom and her whole, "importance of sleep when you're a kid and still growing."

So I tried to just lie there. That's when I realized my dog knew exactly what I was feeling.

Thump.

He was trying to tell me he was still there.

Thump.

He was trying to tell me he would always be there.

Like a heartbeat. *Thump thump thump thump thump.*

If that isn't magic, you tell me.